This star belongs to

....

....

....

....

BARNEY'S
Big Spring Clean

Story by Peter Bonnici
Pictures by Lisa Kopper
From an original idea by Shirley-Anne Lewis

A Magnet Book

It was a warm Spring morning and Roger the mouse had started his scratching season. This was a problem, because Roger lived on top of Barney's head and the scratching kept Barney awake at night.

Barney yawned and stretched as he made his
sleepy way down to breakfast. Roger scratched and
scratched. It was a particularly itchy scratch –
behind his ears, under his chin, down his back.

   He turned and twisted and bumped and scratched,
and his tail flopped down onto Barney's nose.

"That tickles," yelled Barney.

Too late . . .

His nose twitched and crinkled up and a huge
sneeze escaped; "A-A-T-I-S-H-O-O-O!"

It was such a huge sneeze that Barney lost his balance
and fell, head first, bumping down the stairs.

He lay sprawled on his back staring
up at the ceiling. It was spinning round
and round and there, swinging from
the light, was poor old Roger, who was
most put out at being blown up there.
  "That's disgusting," said Barney.
  "Don't be rude," snapped Roger.
  "I didn't mean you, Roger," said Barney.
"I'm talking about the ceiling."

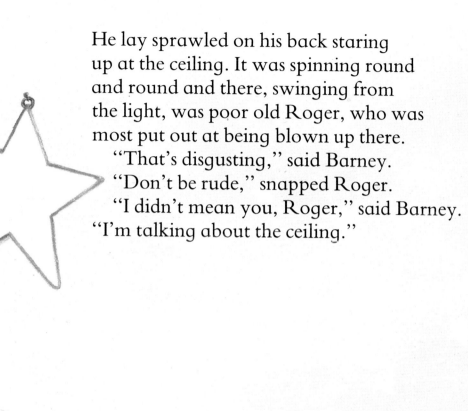

The ceiling was certainly in a bad way, with cobwebs in all the corners and hanging from the lights.
   In fact, everywhere Barney looked, was the same . . . little paw-prints here, little piles of peanut shells there.

"We've got a job to do, old son," said
Barney, in his most Barney voice.

"We . . .?" said Roger. "I keep my little
home very neat and tidy. You haven't had
any complaints about the top of your
head, have you?"

"Tell you what,"
said Barney. "Let's
get Cornelia to help.
She's good at these things.
And besides, she's got a ladder . . ."
   "And buckets," said Roger.
   "And a vacuum cleaner," said Barney.
"In fact, she's got everything we need."

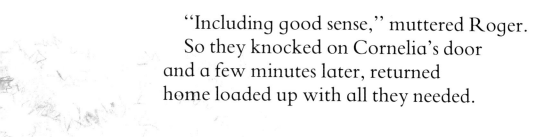

"Including good sense," muttered Roger.
So they knocked on Cornelia's door
and a few minutes later, returned
home loaded up with all they needed.

Cornelia said, "Cover up all the furniture, if you're going to start on the ceiling."

Barney covered the furniture.

"And move everything away from the walls, so that we can have a good go at them," she added.

Barney was already beginning to think that Spring cleaning was a bit too much like hard work.

"Where's that Roger?" he growled.

There came a snore from
under one of the dust sheets.
And then a grunt.
And then another.
And then a lot of rustling
and bumping.

Cornelia gently lifted the
corner of the dust sheet.
There was Roger, half asleep
and scratching away like mad.
  "Lazy creature," barked
Barney. "You're supposed
      to be helping me. Stop
        that scratching
          and come along!"

"Nobody starts Spring cleaning without a plan," said Roger. "And nobody can make a plan without a cup of tea or something."

So the three friends sat down with tea and biscuits to work out their plan.

Cornelia took charge. "Barney, you do the ceiling. Dust the lampshades and then wash them down with a damp rag. Roger, you scrub the doorstep with green soap and hot water."

"And what will you be doing?" asked Barney, suddenly feeling very tired.

"I'll be preparing for the next tea break," said Cornelia.

At that, Barney and Roger cheered up, and started work.

Barney went up the ladder with a long feather brush and fenced away at a very large spider who didn't want her home to be disturbed.

"Cornelia," he called. "Could you hold this for a moment?"

"Certainly, Barney," said Cornelia in her busy little voice.

There was a loud shriek and a crash as she dropped the teapot. Barney, all innocent at the top of the ladder, was handing down to her a long thread of spider web, with the big fat spider still on the end of it!

Roger stood grumpily at the door.

"That's a fine mess you've made there. Thanks."

He stomped back to his job, muttering, "Some of us are happy just to get on with our jobs, and some are happier when they're making a mess."

Soon the sound of gentle scrubbing came from the doorstep.

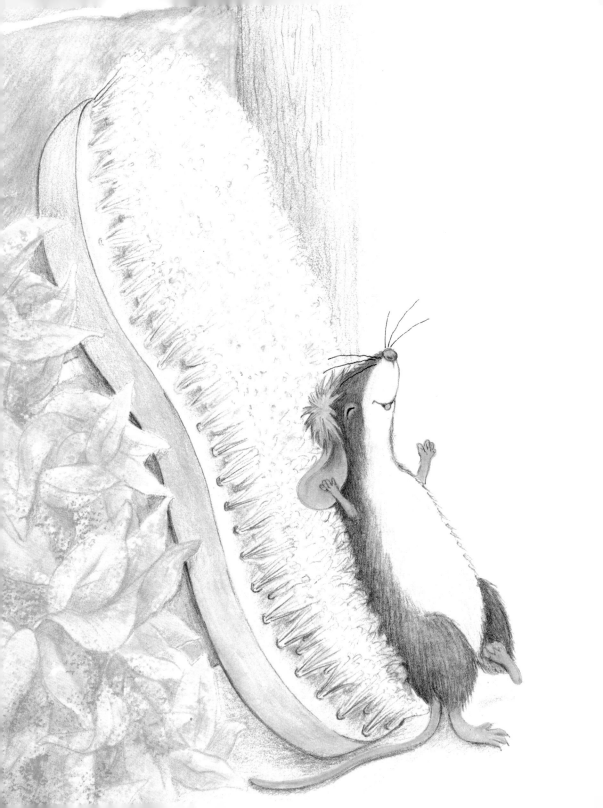

Barney soon finished his dusting and went to get the
bucket of water from Roger. He was most upset to
find the scrubbing sound was not Roger working.
Instead, the brush was leaning up against the wall,
and Roger was scratching his back against it!

Barney snatched the bucket from Roger and
with a growl he gave the soap a hefty kick, then
stomped back to his ladder.

Guess where the soap landed?

By the kitchen door.

And guess who came through the kitchen door with a tray of tea, just as Barney reached the top of his ladder?

Cornelia.

"Tea's up," she started to say, and then she stepped on the soap, and she and the soap and the loaded tea tray flew across the room and landed with a crash against Barney's ladder.

The ladder wobbled.

Barney tried to steady himself. No good.

The ladder and Barney and the bucket of water all came tumbling down.

There was soap and tea and water and biscuits and the ladder all over the carpet.

And on Barney's head . . . the bucket.
  Cornelia gently lifted it off. Before Barney
managed to say even one word, Roger squeaked up.
  "Look on the bright side, Barney. At least *my*
home has had a good Spring clean!"

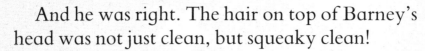

And he was right. The hair on top of Barney's head was not just clean, but squeaky clean!